The
Little
Witch
Sisters

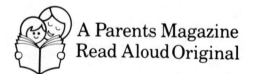

A Parents Magazine
Read Aloud Original

The Little Witch Sisters

by Stephanie Calmenson

pictures by R. W. Alley

Parents Magazine Press • New York

Library of Congress Cataloging-in-Publication-Data

Calmenson, Stephanie.
The little witch sisters / by Stephanie Calmenson;
pictures by R.W. Alley.
    p.   cm.
Summary: Plinka has a surprise for her sister Tinka
when Tinka refuses to help Plinka make a magic brew.
ISBN 0-8193-1191-X
[1. Witches—Fiction.   2. Magic—Fiction.
3. Helpfulness—Fiction.   4. Sisters—Fiction.]
I. Alley, R.W. (Robert W.), ill.   II. Title.
PZ7.C136Lj   1989
[E]—dc19   89-3320
                                                          CIP
                                                          AC

To Jaime and Erica Stechel—S.C.

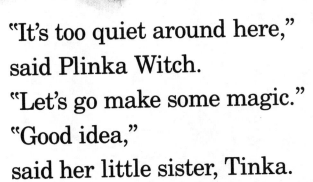

"It's too quiet around here,"
said Plinka Witch.
"Let's go make some magic."
"Good idea,"
said her little sister, Tinka.

Plinka went to make sure
they had the things they needed.
Their hats were nice and pointy.
Their broom was neat and clean.
And their pot was filled with...

"Magic brew!
We're all out of magic brew,"
said Plinka.

"We'll have to make some more.
First we'll need rain water.
Will you do the magic
rain dance with me?"

"I'm busy now," said Tinka.

"Then I will do the magic
rain dance myself,"
said Plinka.
She lifted her cloak
and began tapping her feet.

Swing to the right,
Step one, two, three!
Rainwater please
Fall down to me!

Rain came pouring down.
It filled the pot in no time.
"We need magic mushrooms next,"
said Plinka.
"Will you help me cast the spell?"

"I just remembered
it's time to feed my bats,"
said Tinka, running inside.

"Very well," said Plinka.
"I will cast the spell myself!"
Plinka jumped up and down.
Then she flapped her arms
like a bat and chanted:

Ibbity, jibbity
Bibbety, foo!
Magic mushrooms,
Where are you?

Poof!

A mountain of mushrooms appeared.
They covered Plinka.
As soon as she found her way out,
Plinka dropped three of the biggest
mushrooms into her pot.

"Tinka! We need pumpkin powder!"
called Plinka.
Tinka did not answer.
"Tinka, where are you?"
Plinka called again.
There was still no answer.
Tinka was taking a bubble bath.
She did not hear Plinka calling her.

"I will have to make
the pumpkin powder myself,"
said Plinka.

Plinka dragged a huge pumpkin
into the yard.

Then she took an owl feather
from under her hat,
tickled her nose and whispered:

Achoo! Achoo!
Achibbity-choo!
Pumpkin powder
I need you!

Poof!

Pumpkin powder was everywhere.
"Achoo! Achoo! Achoo!"
sneezed Plinka.
In between sneezes,
Plinka put three big
spoonfuls of powder into her pot.
Then she looked at her recipe.
All the things she needed now
were under her hat:

    3 mugawamp wings
    2 big toe nails
    6 owl feathers
    5 orange gumdrops

Plinka put everything into the pot.
"This is your last chance to help,"
she called.
"We can take turns stirring the brew."
"Yawn," said Tinka,
when she came back from her bath.
"I'll stir first," said Plinka.
While she stirred, she slowly chanted:

Bubble, bubble,
You're in trouble.
If you don't help me
On the double!

"ZZZzzzz," snored Tinka.

By nightfall, the brew was ready.
Tinka woke up and stretched.
"I had such a nice nap," she said.
"And now I am sure you would
like to make magic with me,"
said Plinka.
"Oh, yes!" said Tinka.
"Oh, no!" said Plinka.

"I made the brew by myself,
so I'll make magic by myself too!"
Plinka tossed three drops
of brew on Tinka.

Eenie, meenie,
See you later
Now you are...

"Wait!" cried Tinka.
"Don't leave me this way!"
"All right," said Plinka.

Jingle, jangle,
Have you heard?
Tinka is …

A cuckoo bird!

Poof!

"Oh, no!
I don't want to be a bird either!"
said Tinka.

"But I'm having so much fun,"
said Plinka
And she turned Tinka
into a little, gray elephant.
Even Tinka started to laugh.

But elephants can't fly.
And they can't make magic.
"Please turn me back into a witch.
I promise I'll... I'll..."

"I'll clean up the mess you made!"
said Tinka.
Plinka looked at the yard.
It really was a mess.
"It's a deal," she said.
Plinka tossed three more
drops of brew on Tinka.
Then she said a chant
to undo the spell:

Pop spelled backwards
Still spells pop!
Come back Tinka
Here's the mop!

Poof!

Tinka was a witch again.
She worked hard cleaning the yard,
while Plinka rested.

Finally, when the yard was
all cleaned up,
Plinka and Tinka flew off
into the night.
And...

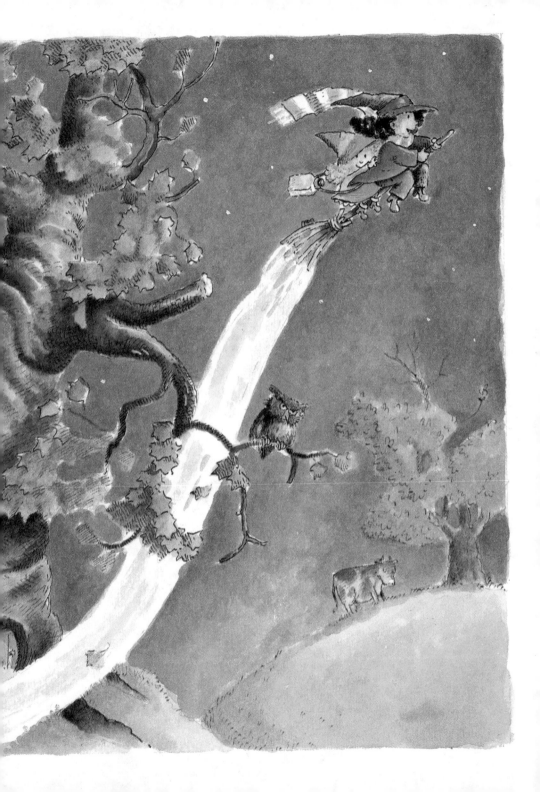

Ibbity, jibbity,
Bibbity, faire.
They made magic
Everywhere!